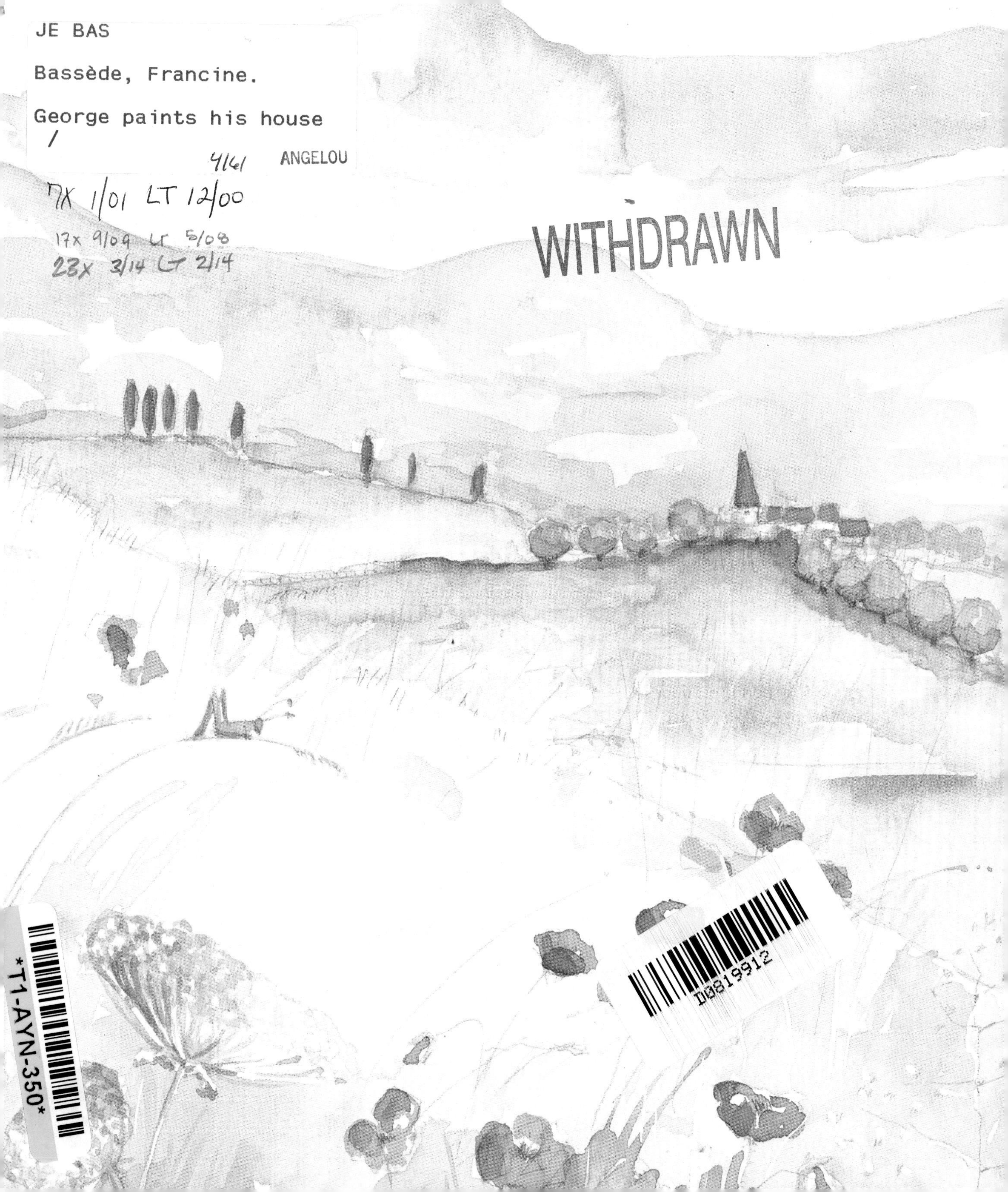

Copyright © 1999 by Siphano, Montpellier
Translation copyright © 1999 by Orchard Books. Translated by Dominic Barth.
First American edition 1999 published by Orchard Books
First published in Great Britain in 1999 by Siphano Picture Books

Orchard Books, A Grolier Company
95 Madison Avenue, New York, NY 10016

Manufactured in the United States of America
Printed and bound by Phoenix Color Corp.
Book design by Mina Greenstein
The text of this book is set in 18 point Veljovic Book.
The illustrations are watercolor reproduced in full color.
10 9 8 7 6 5 4 3 2 1

Library of Congress Cataloging-in-Publication Data
Bassède, Francine. [Georges repeint sa maison. English]
George paints his house / by Francine Bassède ;
[translated by Dominic Barth]. —1st American ed.   p.   cm.
Summary: George and his friend Mary get lots of suggestions on the best color
to paint his house.
ISBN 0-531-30150-8 (trade : alk. paper).—ISBN 0-531-33150-4 (lib. : alk. paper)
[1. Color—Fiction.   2. House painting—Fiction.]   I. Barth, Dominic.   II. Title.
PZ7.B29285Gd 1999 [E]—dc21 98-30531

George Paints His House

Francine Bassède

Orchard Books • New York

George is going to repaint his house—
it's about time! His good friend Mary comes
to help. But what color paint should they
choose? George and Mary can't decide. . . .

Yellow? Like the sun or the mimosa flowers they gather in the fields by the armful?

"Yes," says the lizard, "yellow is luminous, the most lovely of all colors!"

Red? Like poppies, or geraniums, or cherries picked in the spring?

"But of course," say the ladybugs. "Red is joyful, a splendid color!"

Blue? Like cornflowers or the sky?
"Wonderful," sings the bluebird. "Blue is
the color of dreams."

Black or white?
"Black!" says the bull.

"White!" says the horse. "Black *and* white," says the magpie. "They go very well together!"

Or maybe orange? Like apricots and oranges, and the tasty marmalade made from them!

"And like me," says Mary.

Perhaps purple? Like figs, and irises, and delicious grapes?

"Obviously," says the butterfly. "It would be most original of you!"

Pink, do you think? Like the graceful flamingos George photographs in the summer? Or like the hydrangea that grows in the garden?

"I like pink," says Mary.

Why not green, like the banks of the brook where George and Mary fish under the willow tree?

"Green! Green! Green!" croaks the frog. "Like limeade!"

After much discussion, George and Mary
agree on green, and to celebrate, they throw
a party . . .

. . . to thank everyone who
helped—such good friends!

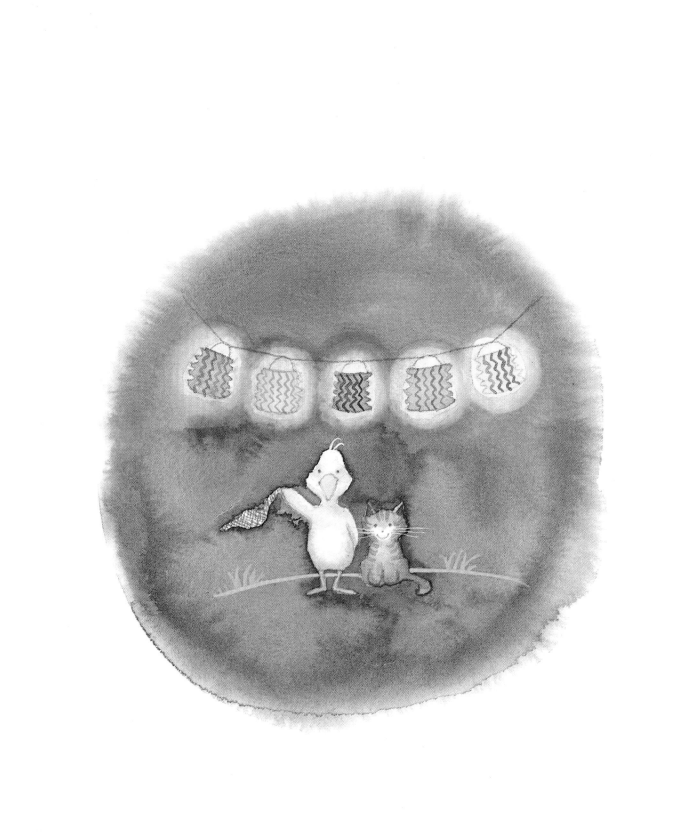